The Stoat Rebellion
by Aubrey Fossedale

A Michael Roach Book
Illustrations by Felicity Roma Bowers

Acknowledgements:

Many thanks to:

Woodland Creatures
Verli the Vole
Mingo Waterwell of Mingo's Yard, Bedminster, Bristol
Jervaise Ticklefish, Southbank Woodland Arts, London SE1
Morteki Ben Adam Brock
Jimmy the Vole
Dorian James of Dorian James Boutiques and Fashion Warehouse
Vince Tatlock of Tatlock's Yard, Salford Quays, Manchester
Harry The Juice of Bethnal Green, East London
Dave Juice
Sir Mungo Robinson, Head of Woodland Independent Television

Humans
Robert W. Palmer
Felicity Roma Bowers

Published 2011
Text © Michael Roach
Illustrations © Felicity Roma Bowers

Available from www.lulu.com
ISBN: 978-1-4467-7844-9

This book is dedicated to Bogle McFarland the pacifist stoat poet who in September 1970 was tried and sentenced to death by an emergency military court of the Woodland Central Government Army at Rochester in Kent for publishing his poem, "What, went my merry dew" which was deemed to be an act of treason.

Bogle McFarland was hanged until pronounced dead by members of the 1st Battalion, 6th Airborne Regiment, Section 22, W.C.G.A at Rochester Barracks at 7.30 am on the 20th October 1970. Hanging was abolished in the New English Democratic Woodland in 1980. May Pan go with him.

What, went my merry dew

What, went my merry dew

In field and furrow
land has turned
brown and red
with the blood of folly foot
and reckless paw.

Unpicked crop
and harsh voices
on concrete
with brass buckle
and the might
of a rifle butt
wriggle as the trench tin
through the autumn sunshine
which shines like a sun dial
on the rows of a once hungry
and DDT scarred dead.

What, went my merry dew

On fettered bow
and row of hedge
lie the shreds of clothing
which were not for comfort
or for show.

The rags tell tales
of mortality and blood shed.
A cat walk of carnage
endured only
by the masses.

What, went my merry dew

Bogle McFarland, stoat poet,
March 1949–October 1970

Contents

Foreword

The English woodland is now run on a democratic system which was fought for during the Stoat Rebellion. The rebellion, fought between the Woodland Central Government Army and the Stoat Rebel Army involved many battles, stalemates and political meetings that had effect on the way the woodland was run, both then and now. In recent times there has been much discussion of the now disbanded Section 22, WCGA, who were accused of atrocities at the relief of Weaselville and during the fighting in Northumberland. This book attempts to resolve any myths or legends about the events that took place during the rebellion. Also it documents the strategies and tactics of both the WCGA and SRA from 1965 – 1977. Both North Somerset and Northumberland are fascinating places in England which saw both heavy troop movements and fighting.

Somerset. The 'Sumorsaete' recorded in the Anglo-Saxon Chronicle and remembered in the motto of Somerset Woodland County were, so the language experts tell us, 'the creatures of the summer lands'. The weasels, stoats and voles, who were here before the Saxons, called it Gwlad yr haf, which means 'land of summer'. So the Saxons invading these parts in the later 7th century described the area as the native creatures described it before them. The sun shining on the bright green spring grass of the Levels can be seen clearly from across the Bristol Channel, and it is perhaps that which so struck those who lived here so long ago. Acres of green marshlands spreading deep inland meant that winter floods were over and rich summer grazing would soon be available. It was the land which came into its own in the summer, and the name the new owners gave to their principal settlement was appropriately the summer town, Somerton.

Northumberland. The distinctive rounded Cheviot Hills were formed when lava erupted from the earth's core and flowed out over the area. The hills are criss-crossed with bridleways which allow weasels, stoats and voles to follow the routes of ancient goat drovers. The dramatic waterfall of Linhope Spout is worth a visit for creatures, as is the ascent to the highest point in Northumberland, Cheviot Summit, from where the Pennine snakes along the border ridge. At the Cheviots' northern edge, you can still trace the hut circles left within the pre-Roman site of Yeavering Bell.

The following pages are the result of exciting research and interviews by Aubrey Fossedale who was born in a modest burrow in Soho, London. His early years were spent as a typesetter for the Woodland Times. At the outset of the rebellion he joined the City of Westminster Vole Regiment with whom he fought at the relief of Weaselville, after which he was posted to a forward unit of his regiment in the Cheviot Hills in Northumberland. After his demobilisation Aubrey gained a post at Woodland Independent Television where he is employed as a script writer in the light entertainment department. Aubrey is also on the steering committee of the Dilettantes' Ball, which is a popular annual event for arts orientated voles who fought the rebellion for their arts freedom and suffered from being called passé and having to work in outreach positions. Aubrey enjoys many friends from all walks of life and regularly dines with myself and his Grace the Reverend Septimus Wilkinson, the Bishop of Matabeleland.

Jervaise Ticklefish, Head of South Bank Woodland Arts

Chapter One

The Road to Rebellion

1960

With a blinding flash and click, the lamps came on and the pistols were cocked as Corporal Arthur Jenkins of the British Woodland Army stood with bare paws on a cold and wet East Berlin street waiting to be exchanged for the Soviet woodland double agent André Goonavitch. Arthur had been spying for the Woodland Government at a shilling week extra pay but had been caught in the act. Instead of being tortured by the Soviet Woodland Secret Police, who knew only too well the life of a stoat from the North of England, they showed him a world where there wasn't any religion and all creatures were equal. Both creatures walked nervously to their respective sides and that was it; Arthur was free after spending two years in the Soviet Creatures' Socialist Republic, but with a very different point of view from the one he had before. As he traveled back in the cart to headquarters he could overhear his officers sitting at the front talking. "Why do we use stoats for our operations in East Berlin?" one said. The only reply was "Because they are mostly expendable". By 1963 Arthur had come in from the cold and was demobbed back to the North of England and the back- breaking work that he had left ten years earlier in search of something better.

Since time immemorial the weasels, stoats and voles of woodland society had lived side by side in peace and harmony. But by the end of 1964, bitter injustices that had simmered at the heart of that tranquil and stable community were about to boil over into a long, bloody and cruel conflict that was to have far reaching consequences. As 1964 started the woodland community was very much the same as it had always been. Stoats and weasels were living and working together but not entirely on an equal basis. The élite of the woodland, as ever, enjoyed all the trappings of wealth and power. However, the ever growing stoat equality movement, led by the now demobbed Arthur Jenkins in the North of England, was gathering more and more momentum and finally spilled over into action during the merry month of May in that year. A stoat named Sidney Leafbuckle was sacked for refusing to run the belt in a tailor's shop in the town of Chorley in Lancashire. Running the belt was the only job that stoats were offered in the woodland rag trade and they never could or would be tailors or cutters. Sidney refused and, on picking up a pair of scissors, had been sacked. This small incident led to over 50,000 stoats marching in to Rotherham town centre in South Yorkshire to meet with Arthur Jenkins. As stoat leaders went he was gritty, genuine and ex-Woodland Army Intelligence Corps. He had been in the orphanage as a kitten and worked in the yards where the gentle woodland folk still don't go. Arthur was also very charismatic and had a woodland charm that could not be bought even with Welsh gold. As the 50,000 arrived in front of him he held a human shot gun above his head and said these famous words. "Happen we will get what we want by the use of any means at our disposal". As he said this a cheer went up and word soon traveled. By June nearly all the stoats in the Woodland Army had mutinied and were heading North. In fact nearly every stoat in the south of England was heading for Rotherham.

The Stoat Rebel Army was soon formed and its respective regiments were coming to the fore; Salford 101, Tyne and Weir 42, Middlesborough 56. The most notorious of these were Salford 101 who were highly politically motivated. In the south the Woodland Army, who were now in disarray, were being re-organised by their commander General John Acorn, a weasel who had been in the Woodland Army since World War I. The formation of the Woodland Central Government Army could been seen as a hurried affair by many, and General Acorn could be criticised for this, however woodland society had fallen and both sides were facing an all out civil war, as well as frequent indiscriminate attacks by the human population with DDT that were killing all and sundry across the nation. The élite were not on his side either. They had fled to collective farms to avoid violence which left General Acorn and Arthur Jenkins with hundreds of thousands of poor and middle ground creatures on each side. The WCGA quickly came under the directive of six paw-picked, bowler-hatted voles who were the remnants of woodland government, now the élite had gone, to assist the intellectual weasel Cornelius Wartbury in governing the weasel and vole population in southern England. The plan was that each vole would minister and administer each sector of the south; Wessex, Essex, the Medway and Henley-on-Thames, the Home Counties and Brighton (inclusive of Margate). All creatures love Margate – its where they spend their holidays in the summer.

This stroke of genius worked. The WCGA, who were still fighting a sort of phony rebellion at this point, were delivering gas masks to all. Injuries and deaths were low and things were going well. Back in the North things were going even better for the newly formed SRA which had nearly one million recruits; however, these creatures had to be fed and clothed. The SRA started to ship in uniforms and rations from the stoat population on the Isle of Man, who had set up factories there to aid the SRA. The civilian population on the mainland were starting to receive education and food as well. In a matter of months both sides were preparing for the biggest confrontation the British woodland had ever seen. By the Christmas and Ticklemas of that year nothing had happened because basically nothing happens at this time of the year apart from feasting and merriment and who wants to interrupt that?

In March 1965 the main attack came. Arthur Jenkins' mutineer stoat rebel army were moving south with 500,000 creatures in the front line and the same in reserve. Everything in their path was being eaten up by the might of their marching paws. In reality their uniforms and kit were obsolete and their rifles and artillery were out of date. Their weaponry was no match for the WCGA artillery catapult batteries that had radar and a never ending supply of hot and cold rounds. But for now the stoats were winning and advancing at such a rate that the WCGA were not able to withdraw fast enough and were suffering heavy casualties. At this point the yards had not joined in with the rebellion and believed that even though the SRA were advancing it would still not affect them as they employed all creatures on an equal basis. Mingo's Yard, Harry the Juice and Tatlock's in the North, who were stoats, were holding back. Their claim was that most of them had been in the Woodland Army anyway and in many ways they just weren't interested. Nevertheless, the stoats were on the march and all had to watch out. Weaselville prepared for the worst, but how can you measure what is the worst if it has not happened yet? North Somerset at this point had been virtually untouched by the war but the SRA were closing in and what was a busy city in a quiet back water was to become what has been held by both historians and intellectuals alike as the cradle of the entire conflict.

With trenches dug in the suburbs and the civilian population moved back towards its centre, the city drew a deep breath in preparation for the SRA's arrival. On May 2nd the SRA took up positions five miles from Weaselville's suburbs. At the front were the infantry armed with .101 rifles and to the rear was the artillery. SRA artillery at that time was a strange affair; human shot guns, sawn off then mounted on wheels with a pivot that enabled high, low and medium elevation, manned by a crew of eight, then mounted on wheels, all of which was towed by a team of six goats. This type of gun was known at the time as the Pivot Gun and was later taken up by the Woodland Army after all hostilities had ended. Next came the stand off - this went on until May 5th when the stoat infantry attacked. Even though the WCGA had the advantage, the SRA nearly completely surrounded them within seventy two hours. A WAF biplane was dispatched to observe the situation and was shot down by a pivot gun battery. Its crew of two voles, one pilot and one navigator, were captured, tortured and executed by a crack unit of the SRA which sent one of the bodies back to the WCGA lines, strapped to the back of a goat. The weasels then knew that the SRA meant business and also that, apart from one corridor that led to Flax Bourton Airfield and Camp, they were going to be completely surrounded. Weaselville was about to be engaged in a siege that would last for over eighteen months and cost thousands of woodland lives. For the whole of the 5, 6th and 7th of May WCGA Artillery, which were WW2 era catapults with 6-creature crews, pounded the stoat positions. The artillery of the SRA would fire back and attack after attack of the WCGA lines went on. Finally in the end, the WCGA pulled back into a two mile perimeter outside of the city, with a thumb shaped pocket attached that encompassed the airfield and camp. By May 14th stalemate had set in and the siege had begun.

In peace time Weaselville was an unusual place even to the most adventurous creature. Fashionable suburbs around the edge with expensive shops at one end of the city and what could only be deemed as the devil's anvil at the other. East Weaselville was the oldest part of town. It was where all the gambling and prostitution went on. One bar, the Sai Jean, was to take centre stage in the oncoming siege and rebellion that would last for nearly 12 years. The Sai Jean was owned and managed by Frankie Waterwell who was, in no uncertain terms, a pimp and crook. As the SRA surrounded them, a tv camera crew and technicians from the newly formed Woodland Independent Television arrived at his door. Most of them were ex WBC, but after the élite had fled at the first sounds of gun fire the WBC had closed its doors. WITV was a brand new station that would keep the news going no matter what. The day tv arrived at the doors of the Sai Jean was the same day that Frankie was interviewing females for bar jobs - after all, he would be expecting a large crowd of punters no matter who won the war. Googie Carmel, who was WITV's only and first female reporter, did not tell Frankie who she was and queued up with the females who were seeking work. As her turn came Frankie told her, after a good inspection by a couple of weasels who looked as though they would sell their own grandmother, that she had made the grade and was in for the late shift. She then announced who she was. Frankie loved it, and her. He said both then and now that she was good enough to work at the Sai Jean. For the next eighteen months WITV made its home in the bar as well as the front line with the infantry and the catapult batteries of the artillery.

Chapter 2

The Woodland Central Government Army

The Woodland Central Government Army was made up of the remnants of the British Woodland Army at the outset of the rebellion. After the Stoat Mutiny the whole organisation had to be changed, with the élite leaving its ranks. Also the nature of training and service was under the spotlight. The Woodland Army had been an effective force since a weasel had knelt beside Wolf at Quebec and had also served at Waterloo, the Indian Mutiny and both world wars. At Dunkirk in 1940 the woodland forces under the command of General Acorn had been rescued by human boats from the beaches after they had destroyed 30 tanks of a Waffen SS Panzer Division. However, in 1965 the human community had turned its back on the woodland, committing open acts of murder on it by dropping air burst DDT. By the end of 1965 the WCGA was very much on its own.

The command structure was decided by Acorn as follows: A series of county regiments, followed up by a large newly expanded airborne brigade and artillery.

Airborne: The 4th, 5th and 6th regiments were expanded to 3, 500 soldiers each, inclusive of the Henley-on-Thames Light Cavalry.

Infantry: County regiments were taken from 100,000 to 200,000 soldiers in strength.

Artillery: Existing catapults in artillery batteries were overhauled and then fitted with modern radio equipment. These were towed by carts with a team of six goats to each. Gaps that had been left by stoats would be filled with the ever hungry line of weasel recruits and all technical artillery duties would be performed by voles who, in the case of airborne artillery, would come from the Henley-on-Thames Light Cavalry and in field artillery cases would come from the City Of Westminster Vole Regiment.

Uniforms: With the whole nature of a rebellion / civil war and changing times the WCGA had to move on from its world war two style battle dress uniforms that had brass shoulder titles and soap pressed creases in all the right places. A brand new uniform was designed by a vole named Dorian James who was fresh out of college and fresh out of luck, with most voles being turned away from the collective farms of the élite. Although this time his luck was in.

Dorian joined the HOTLC in 1966 and was called on from a great height to design a new uniform. Looking at the world around him he chose uniforms that were unlike the British human army and unlike the old Woodland Army. After a lot of deliberation he chose a French uniform with a continental cut and a Portuguese Army camouflage pattern. Dorian placed his designs on the table, which included Red Berets for the Airborne, Black Berets for the Infantry and a rather groovy Royal Blue for the Artillery, all with their respective flashes, including a very striking looking Section 22 shoulder flash. All regiments, no matter who they were, would all wear the same camouflage with bare paws. The powers that be were very impressed and the WCGA had its own uniform. From this uniform legends began.

Training: Was to be as normal, however instruction on each creature's role in a civil war was also given. Civil wars are perilous things and there really are no heroes especially if you're not on the winning side. For the losers your beer is drank and your females are whored. All weasels and voles were given intensive classroom lessons on their position in the greater scheme of things, what the political situation was then, and what it would be like when they had won the rebellion. During the rebellion what was known as jumping the hoop was still in force in all airborne regiments. Every morning during basic training a ring of fire was lit and placed before a trampoline. Cooks would then bring out a hot breakfast which was ready to be served some way from the hoop. Each creature would have to jump through the burning hoop to gain a right to his rations for that day. This practice was not for the faint hearted and was banned in 1980 after being considered an infringement of a creature's right to food whilst serving the woodland. Many creatures, both voles and weasels, still say that the airborne has gone down hill since they banned the practice.

Weaponry: Weasels and voles carried an M2 American-made, fully automatic rifle with an endless supply of 2.6 mm ammunition. These were bought on a lease lend agreement from the American Woodland Military Congress that was headed by General Bugs Weinburger. General Acorn rejected the previous semi-automatic rifle that was in service with the Woodland Army and was quoted as calling it "Fairground Scrap".

Rations: Goon sausage, Tickle Fish, Goon Fish, Baked Beans, Chips with everything

Field Rations: Composition. 1973 post Blackpool peace talks, Airborne Regiments only, Composition Rations plus Hard Tack biscuits and Strawberry Jam, excluding Henley-on-Thames Light Cavalry; Rich Tea biscuits and Apricot Jam.

WCGA Command Structure Status and Order Of Battle at March 1967

General John Acorn; One Bowler-Hatted vole, Ministry of Tactics

4, 5, 6th Airborne Regiments, The Henley-on-Thames Light Cavalry, Section 22

Line Regiments

The Medway Voles; The North Somerset Scratchers; The East London Scratchers; The Cornwall Brigade of Weasels; The East Anglian Berry Pickers; The South London Scratchers; The Gloucester Weasel Brigade; The Home Counties Regiment, inclusive of Knightsbridge and Chelsea Voles Territorial Brigade – known as the Writers and Dandies; The City of Westminster Vole Regiment

Artillery

384 Catapult Field Regiment; 307 Catapult Airborne Regiment, inclusive of the Henley-on-Thames Light Cavalry; 308 Catapult Field Regiment. All regiments except 307 inclusive of the City of Westminster Vole Regiment.

Rear Echelon

The Woodland Central Government Army Service Corps (wheel wrights, bakers, cooks and mobile ablutions companies, inclusive of Henley-on-Thames Light Cavalry clerks attached to section 22)

The Woodland Central Government Army Medical Corps (inclusive of Henley-on-Thames Light Cavalry medics and operating theatre technicians attached to section 22)

302 Training Regiment, Flax Bourton, North Somerset

The Woodland Central Government Army Military Police, voles exempt from service, weasels only.

The command structure showed plainly that the weasels, even though they had invited the voles to share the fighting with them, clearly had the upper paw over military law by the exemption of voles from the Military Police. This was also banned won 1980 and many voles now serve in this as part of what is now the Woodland Democratic Army.

Morality

Some creatures would say that the Woodland has never recovered from the rebellion and the fact that voles and weasels came together as brothers in arms. It was a great social upheaval and many voles from the WCGA would regularly be arrested for drunken and immoral behaviour at the Sai Jean in Weaselville.

In some respects raucous and immoral behaviour would be water off a duck's back to the average airborne weasel, who would drink, fight and take part in the pay-as-you-go sexual services that were on offer at a heavy discount during the rebellion. The Woodland Central Government Army officially took a very strict view on off duty behaviour and had strict guidelines for its soldiers. In reality a blind eye was turned to all of this and mayhem would break out in Weaselville regularly on Friday evenings, whatever WCGA regiment was on leave there.

Chapter 3

The Stoat Rebel Army

The Stoat Rebel Army in 1964 were gaining ground and had thousands of willing recruits from both the North and South of England. Its backbone were regular army stoats who had recently mutinied from the now defunct Woodland Army. Arthur Jenkins centered all training at Bolton in Lancashire. Bolton was a key town for the SRA as it was deep in the North and its rail link connected straight to the Manchester Ship Canal where wounded could be shipped in and troops could be shipped out to stoat held ports in the south of the country. All stoats were recruited into regiments with Yorkshire, Lancashire and Tyneside titles. Also an élite political regiment was formed that later became known as Salford 101. This regiment recruited stoats on the Salford Quays of Manchester who were both from Liverpool and Merseyside. The relationship between the Manchester and Liverpool stoats was disharmonious but together they were a formidable force that engaged the WCGA in many battles over a twelve year period. By early 1965 the Stoat Rebel Army had 500,000 recruits and 500,000 soldiers under its command.

The command structure which follows was decided by Arthur Jenkins and was an élite political force that could take part in field and covert operations which were followed up by infantry, artillery and rear echelon regiments.

The Politicals: Salford 101 Regiment – 50,000 strong inclusive of rear echelon attached regiments.

The Infantry: Tyne and Wear 42; Middlesbrough 56; The Northumberland Stoat Brigade; The Yorkshire and Lancashire Scratchers; The Liverpool and Merseyside Free Stoats.

Artillery: 402 Pivot Gun Field Regiment; 408 Pivot Gun Air Defence Regiment; 490 Pivot Gun Field Regiment (all artillery regiments inclusive of attached rear echelon regiments). All guns in all regiments were fitted with type 19 radio sets and range finding devices. All artillery technical support was given by Stoat volunteers.

Training: The Stoat Rebel Army trained its soldiers in both military skills and in political thought. The training camps deep inside Lancashire taught rigid disciplined military skills such as drill, skill at arms, field craft and map reading but also had time set aside for the improvement of literacy skills and degree-standard qualifications. Most SRA soldiers by 1976 could read and write with many graduating with degrees in political science.

Uniforms: The uniform of the Stoat Rebel Army was designed and made by the stoat population of the Isle of Man. It was the mark of a true rebel. All soldiers in all regiments, including the politicals, were issued with olive drab fatigues and winter weather parkas with bare paws. Fatigue caps were the same colour for all regiments. A Che Guevara motif was worn on all caps. Shoulder flashes denoting regimental numbers, e.g. 101, 56, 408 AD, were worn on all jackets.

Weaponry: .101 bolt action rifles were bought and shipped in from North Africa. These rifles held a clip of five rounds that were loaded through the breach when the bolt was pulled back into the magazine, which was positioned underneath the rifle. Crack units of the SRA could fire thirty rounds per minute at the height of the rebellion. The rifles had a wooden stock usually made from mahogany or walnut. Ammunition was plentiful, however stocks would deplete when cargo boats were sunk on the approach to the United Kingdom.

Rations: Goon Sausage, Tickle Fish, Goon Fish, Baked Beans, Chips with everything. 1973 post Blackpool peace talks onwards, Bread and Dripping every other Monday.

Field Rations: Composition.

Stoat Rebel Army Command Structure Status and Order Of Battle at April 1965

Arthur Jenkins, Chief of Stoat General Staff

Stoat General Staff; Four Regular Army Stoats, Four Political Stoats

Salford 101 Regiment Political Wing

Salford 101 Regiment Field Companies

Line Regiments

Tyne and Weir 42; Middlesborough 56; The Northumberland Stoat Brigade; The Yorkshire and Lancashire Scratchers; The Liverpool and Merseyside Free Stoats.

Artillery

402 Pivot Gun Field Regiment; 408 Pivot Air Defence Regiment; 490 Pivot Gun Field Regiment (all artillery regiments inclusive of attached rear echelon regiments)

Rear Echelon

The Stoat Rebel Army Medical Service; 48 Regiment General Hospital, Bolton, Lancashire

The Stoat Rebel Army Service Corps (bakers, wheel rights, clerks, mobile ablutions companies)

The Stoat Rebel Army Military Police and Internal Affairs Department

432 Training Regiment, Bolton, Lancashire

Internal Affairs Department

Restricted under 1977 Stoat Rebel Army end of rebellion act, sub section para. c.

Morality

Unlike the WCGA the morality of the Stoat Rebel Army was high, however because of the lack of opportunity of most stoats, theft was ever present. Shipments of guns and ammunition could often be tampered with and have items missing on arrival or in transit. Some stoats caught in acts of theft were imprisoned for this, however many cases were hard to solve so the Internal Affairs Department was set up in 1974 to deal with this problem. The department, who still run, are now a part of the Woodland Democratic Army and their records are closed to the public.

Chapter 4

Section 22

As the siege of Weaselville went on, pressure increased on General Acorn to gain ground and bring about the relief of the city. After a long meeting with Cornelius Wartbury and the vole ministers it was decided to create a sub-government department named Section 22. Its aim was to recruit, deliver and train soldiers of the WCGA for the newly expanded airborne regiments. Acorn knew that the siege could not be ended without this and that he had also to create corridors in the stoat lines, firstly, by sending the already battle weary remnants of his army that were defending the city into action once again. By January 1967 the corridors had been captured and weasels living in battle free areas could travel to the city without much hindrance, although SRA artillery still rained down at regular intervals. In February Acorn took one of his most controversial decisions of the entire conflict and created a mandate that all scrap yard workers and released prisoners from Her Majesty's Woodland Prison at Swindon would be eligible to join the army. Once the call had been put out creatures turned up by the thousand to receive the shilling.

The woodland press, who were still operating at the time, had a field day and reported that Acorn's Troopers would massacre the stoats. A paw-drawn cartoon on the front of the Woodland Times depicted a woodland trooper with a bag of swag standing over the body of a dead stoat. Acorn's only answer to this was that the free press would do half his work for him and to let the SRA see this and fully digest it. In March Section 22 was administering the training of mainly airborne recruits at Flax Bourton airfield. The third airborne regiment had swelled in its ranks from 500 to 1500 in this time, with regular army and hostilities-only volunteers rubbing shoulders together. Into the ranks of the airborne also came the Henley-on-Thames Light Cavalry. In 1965 the HOTLC were a run-down Territorial Unit who had last seen action at Suez where they had had made the last cavalry charge of the British Woodland Army but, because of bungling by successive human governments, they were left only with a Nissen hut, 6 tired goats and one trooper armed only with a telephone.

The Henley-on-Thames area had suffered badly with human drops of DDT. The woodland population there were mainly voles who were starving and badly in need of care. Most females and kittens were taken to the safety of London but nearly all males of working age were left to starve. Seeing this, Acorn noticed that there was recruiting potential there - but how was he going to attract the voles? These were peace loving creatures. They wrote poetry and made wine and were not interested in armies or any kind of war. A meeting of Ministers was held and it was decided that yes, voles were peace loving and unlikely to join, but in peace time they were treated as secondary by the élite, who considered their art work to be passé. Also, they were only given outreach jobs and were never classed as part of mainstream arts, only the fringe, so why not offer them control of woodland arts once the rebellion had been won? The élite, who controlled the judiciary, the arts and television had fled, leaving a gap for the voles to move into, providing they joined the WCGA and fought the war. This proved to be successful and voles volunteered in their thousands.

The HOTLC was given regimental status and re-roled as an airborne regiment. To attract the voles it would keep its name and all its traditions. The first voles arrived at Flax Bourton Airfield in March 1966, however the most famous, Jervaise Ticklefish, did not arrive until later in the year. Section 22, which was full of hard-nutted and ex-con weasels, were about to rub shoulders with the middle ground of the English woodland. Two cultures with two aims, two cap badges, but after 6 weeks airborne training, lots of common ground. At first the weasels and voles hated each other, one side seeing the other as crass and vice versa, but after a few weeks it all settled down. The HOTLC were to fill the gaps where radio operators, medics and operating theatre technicians were needed. The HOTLC would not fight as a regiment but were to be embedded into every section of every company of the entire WCGA airborne.

There are many stories and legends of Section 22, most of which are fiction but some of which are fact. Section 22 were instrumental in the twelve year fight against the SRA and were the lead soldiers deployed in Northumberland from 1968–1977. Soldiers who were recruited by this department, which no longer exists, were members of the airborne first and had the department stamped in their pay book. The Woodland Democratic Army still refuses to talk about this department and still say that it was a government administrative department and not a part of the army. However, every creature that has served in it has always said that they were Section 22 before anything else. A former soldier of the SRA who was interviewed on the Woodland Channel some time ago said that he fought Section 22 units of the woodland airborne regularly. The department's most famous recruit was Morteki Ben Adam Brock (Brocky the Weasel) who was recruited from Mingo's Yard, Bristol in 1967 at 19 years old. Brocky, as he was known, fought mainly in Northumberland during the 1970's and distinguished himself as a primary soldier of the woodland airborne.

Chapter 5

The Relief of Weaselville

June 14th 1966

The newly expanded WCGA airborne regiments were fully trained and ready to deploy against the Stoat Rebel Army that surrounded Weaselville. The Woodland Air Force, who only had a few small biplanes, were short of pilots and aircraft, though. The call went out for vole volunteers to train as pilots. This call was received with great attention and voles queued in their hundreds. The Woodland Air Force was very set in its ways in 1965 and its command were welcoming the new DC1 aircraft but not the volunteer voles, some of whom were rejecting the detachable collars that they were issued. In a very short space of time though, things improved and by July 16th 1966 all aircraft pilots and soldiers were ready for the relief of the woodland's most famous city.

Order of Battle WCGA, WAF, July 16th 1966, Flax Bourton Airfield, North Somerset

First wave, airborne forces, No2 Squadron WAF

5, 6th Airborne Regiments, The Henley-on-Thames Light Cavalry – Section 22; 307 Catapult Airborne Regiment inclusive of the Henley-on-Thames Light Cavalry

Second Wave, Ground Forces

The South London Scratchers; The Writers and Dandies; The City of Westminster Vole Regiment; The Home Counties Regiment; The Cornwall Brigade of Weasels; The Woodland Central Government Army Service Corps (wheel wrights, bakers, cooks and mobile ablutions companies, inclusive of Henley-on-Thames Light Cavalry clerks attached to section 22)

The Woodland Central Government Army Medical Corps (inclusive of Henley-on-Thames Light Cavalry medics and operating theatre technicians attached to section 22); The Woodland Central Government Army Military Police.

Held in reserve

4th Airborne Regiment; The North Somerset Scratchers; The East London Scratchers; The East Anglian Berry Pickers; The Gloucester Weasel Brigade.

0500 hrs: Two hundred and fifty DC1 aircraft took off from Flax Bourton Airfield with over seven thousand airborne troopers within them.

0600hrs: The WAF aircraft had reached their drop zone, which was five miles behind enemy lines at Weaselville.

0605hrs: Acorn's Troopers started to make their drop. The sight of seven thousand soldiers descending from the air must have been terrifying to the stoats on the ground.

0608hrs: All airborne units were deployed on the ground, all drop zones were secured and defended.

0610hrs: The ground forces advanced through the thumb-shaped pocket, heavy fighting started and the SRA opened up with a salvo from 490 Pivot Gun Regiment. The South London Scratchers suffered heavy casualties but the advance carried on.

0630hrs: The airborne troopers, now on paw, started to close on the stoat lines in a pincer movement, the 5th to right and the 6th to the left.

0700hrs: Heavy fighting, almost paw-to-paw combat, broke out between the 5th Airborne and Salford 101 Regiment. Both stoats, weasels and voles suffered heavy casualties.

0710hrs: Air and ground forces met and surrounded all SRA units.

0730hrs: WCGA airborne artillery fired a salvo of hot coals, which rained down on the Yorks and Lancs Scratchers. The Yorks and Lancs counter attacked and committed a near slaughter of the Home Counties Regiment.

0750hrs: The Yorks and Lancs Scratchers opened a corridor in the WCGA lines that led to Portishead, a small port on the coast of North Somerset.

0800hrs: All Stoat Rebel Army regiments were surrounded from their advance and retire positions.

The WCGA had suffered from medium casualties. The SRA, who suffered huge casualties, organised a withdrawal through what has become known to this day as the Portishead corridor.

0845hrs: Whilst being pounded by WCGA artillery fire and suffering continuous attacks, the SRA commander Colonel Jingles Nettle then sent a signal to SRA, GHQ in Bolton, Lancashire.

0900hrs: GHQ Bolton replied and ordered Nettle to withdraw to Portishead. The orders were to hold the port until the hospital ship, the Pride of the Tyne had reached there. Estimated time of arrival after leaving its berth at Salford Quays was two days.

0930hrs: Weaselville was relieved and the bells rang out for Victory.

0945hrs: The WCGA forces had secured Weaselville.

After 10 am on July 16th the WCGA had won all but one of its objectives of the day. What lay ahead in the fighting and defending of Portishead and its corridor became one of the most controversial periods of the whole rebellion.

The Portishead Corridor

On the July 17th the battle was won, but there were still pockets of fighting outside the suburbs and around a perimeter that had been set up by the Stoat Rebel Army. The perimeter was one mile in depth and defended by elements of Salford 101 regiment. Two thirds of the SRA were heading North towards Bristol then on to their main objective of Stroud, where they would rejoin their transport units and withdraw to the North of the country. The regiments that had been held in reserve by the WCGA were deployed against the SRA who were heading North, while the air and ground forces that had been fighting the siege were then engaged against the SRA that were holding the perimeter of the Portishead Corridor. After twelve hours the SRA perimeter pulled back and the WCGA advanced, putting 307 Catapult Airborne Regiment into action again against the retreating stoats. The artillery barrage by 307 damaged the perimeter but it still held. The stoats of Tyne and Wear 42 Regiment and Salford 101 were fighting for their lives at this point. To the stoats' amazement they were joined by thousands of civilian stoats who were living in the area. These were mostly females and kittens who had survived the human DDT drops. Salford 101 held the perimeter whilst Tyne and Wear 42 organised the withdraw of the civilians. Thousands of stoats were heading for Portishead dock. When Tyne and Wear 42 reached the dock the Pride of the Tyne was still a day away from arriving. Salford 101 were holding what was now an ever decreasing perimeter with high casualties. The WCGA were bringing even more catapult regiments from their reserve that were closing in range of the dock. During this period the woodland artillery on the vole and weasel side used hot coals as their main ammunition. Each catapult, that was directed by voles in a front position, electrically fired three rounds simultaneously. The power of these weapons in a woodland war was unimaginable. Glowing red-hot coals would rain down on troops, civilians and buildings alike, causing a fire storm at their point of impact. Tyne and Wear 42 set to work organising the wounded and the civilians on the dock. More and more females and kittens were arriving, with hundreds still traveling through the corridor, when the first catapult round hit one of the wharfs. As the perimeter decreased in size even more, the WCGA increased its fire power towards the dock. Nearly all of its artillery regiments were deployed against Portishead. The scene on the dock was one of near atrocity with the wounded laying next to the dead, soldiers trying to put out fires and females trying to shelter their kittens in a hopeless attempt against the constant shelling. The SRA were nearly driven into the sea. As luck would have it the WCGA artillery were becoming low on ammunition. More coals had to be brought in from the Forest of Dean and this would take at least twenty four hours. As well as this, SRA units were withdrawing but still fighting in that area. Salford 101 were managing to hold the perimeter and Tyne and Wear 42 set up an emergency hospital on the dock, that was now a charred mess of wharfs and buildings. The arrival of the hospital ship was only twenty four hours away.

The next day was one of fierce fighting on the perimeter with the advance and then withdrawal of Salford 101. On July 19th the *Pride of the Tyne* sailed into Portishead dock. A huge cheer went up from the six thousand stoats who were still alive - safety was in sight. As the hospital ship moored, the SRA and civilian wounded were carried to the edge of the dock and those who were fit and able stood in orderly queues waiting to board the ship. As the stoats were boarding, the WCGA artillery resumed firing. This caused panic and the stoats ran across the dock shouting, *"Acorn's troopers are going to kill us!"*. This wasn't far from the truth as the WCGA were not far away and the artillery rounds were landing again with even greater accuracy. All of a sudden a female ran to the bridge of the ship and sang into the tannoy the song, "The night they drove old Dixie down". This echoed throughout the blazing port. Soldiers, wounded and civilians were being killed again as they queued on the dock. Out of six thousand creatures only four thousand made it to the ship. The scene was one of carnage. The engines of the ship started up and with its stern on fire the *Pride of the Tyne* sailed into the safety of the Severn estuary. Salford 101 were still fighting on the dock as it left. Their perimeter withdrew but never broke. Very few creatures from this unit got away, the rest were taken prisoner and sent to deep inside Somerset for the duration of the rebellion. Two thirds of the SRA had now reached Stroud in Gloucestershire. Their transport had been secured and with a large part of the WCGA behind them, and some of their units still fighting as a rear guard, they left for the North. Legend has it that they were beaten back twenty five miles North of Birmingham, but in reality they headed for Shropshire, where one of their logistics camps was situated, and then finally left in September for Rotherham and Bolton, where they regrouped for the next fight which would be a ten year guerrilla-style war in Northumberland.

When asked by the woodland press about the atrocities committed by relentless artillery fire on an army that included civilians, Acorn's answer was this;

"Arthur Jenkins had declared that all stoats had left the South of England to join their comrades in the North, so how could there be any atrocity when there were no civilians in that area? Also, the use of artillery is necessary in any conflict". In 1970 the WCGA blew up Clevedon Pier to prevent any further escape route for the SRA should the occasion arise.

Chapter 6

Another Way

As the *Pride of the Tyne* left Portishead dock with its stern on fire no one noticed the small weasel cargo boat that steamed out alongside it bound for New York. On board were a small band of weasels and stoats who rejected violence and saw music as a way out of the fighting. Their boat, the *Africa Shell*, was taking them away from the war and to a land of opportunity. The North Atlantic is a difficult crossing for any boat and as the waves battered the *Africa Shell* the creatures inside had to hang on for dear life itself. There were many times between Portishead and New York that they thought the boat would capsize and they would all be drowned, but in August of 1966 the *Africa Shell* finally docked at New York. To the creatures' amazement they were met by the US Woodland Police, the press and the Immigration Authorities who placed them in quarantine. They were questioned for hours by the police about why they had left civil war torn England, why they didn't want to fight and what they were doing in the United States. After two weeks of confinement the creatures' spokesman came forward - a weasel by the name of Chives. He told the authorities in New York that he and the other weasels and stoats were a band that played modern jazz and they could not find it within their hearts to fight and kill other creatures. He said that they had starved in the famine and escaped the DDT drops and nearly lost their lives on the dock at Portishead where they had helped with the civilian stoats and the wounded. The authorities deliberated on this and allowed them to stay.

Chives and his band were now in New York City with no money and nowhere to stay. They bumped into a gopher on Broadway who directed them to Carnegie Hall where they were hiring cleaners. On arrival they met with a Beaver named Ruben who was a fast talking New Yorker. He gave Chives and his friends a broom each and told them to start work immediately. Ruben also said they could live under the stage, but they had to be quiet during the concerts. So there it was - Chives and his band had survived the stoat rebellion and made it to New York. Working at the hall was no mean feat; it was a twelve hour day on very low money, but Chives would still encourage his band to practice their favourite tune, which was Work Song. In some ways this became their signature tune over the next few months. The band's late night practice sessions were starting to get noticed. The band's repertoire had become larger and creatures from the city were coming in to the hall just to listen. By the end of the year, Chives had his band up and running and playing My Funny Valentine and Apple Core as the centre piece of their late night sets. Ruben the Beaver was noticing all of this and saw potential in the band and called a friend of his, named Herb the Gopher, who was a plugger in the city. He invited Herb to come along one night and listen to the band. From his arrival Herb was sold on the sound from England, but he did warn Chives that if he and his band made it big they would have both the English and American Woodland press up behind them. Herb pointed out that while creatures were fighting and dying in England Chives could be seen as having one long party. Chives listened to this and replied *"There has to be another way"*. Herb was in agreement - he was also an artist and was not the type to join in with violence in any shape or form.

Herb, Ruben, Chives and his band all set to work organising a gig and writing an album. The album's name was to be *Weaselville*. All the creatures knew this would be slammed by the press but they had an ace up their sleeve.

The band's line up was as follows:

Chives' Band, The 1967 Weaselville Album

Ruben Greenstein, Beaver, Manager

Chives McGregor, Weasel , Piano

Stevie McGraph, Stoat, Double Bass

Herb the Gopher, American Gopher, Flute, Plugger

Chick Williams, Stoat, Trombone

Bogle Jenkins, Weasel, Trumpet

Ginger Jones, Stoat, Drums

The 1967 line up was quite something and all members contributed to the writing of *Weaselville*. The album was to consist of eleven tracks, with a cover that would be very boring but quickly changed when the press were on their heels.

The tracks then and now are as follows:

Weaselville

Greenstein, McGregor, McGraph, Herb, T, G, Williams, Jenkins, Jones

01 Lullaby of Birdland

02 Take the 'A' Train

03 Nature Boy

04 My Funny Valentine

05 Work Song

06 Softly as in a Morning Sunrise

07 Take Five

08 African Flower

09 Apple Core

10 Have You Met Miss Stoat

11 Sonny's Blues

In January 1968 *Weaselville* was launched on the American Woodland Label. In the United States it sold like there was no tomorrow, however across the Atlantic there was a different reaction. As expected the British woodland press had reacted very badly.

The head line across the Woodland Times read:

"While Chives Lives it Up in New York, Creatures Meet Their Maker"

The column with the headline then went on to ask how could anyone call their album *Weaselville* when they weren't from the poverty that was there. The British woodland press had damned it and said it wasn't genuine. Ruben told the band to wait until the Rolling Stone magazine review was published which he knew would be far kinder, then play the ace that was up their sleeve.

The Rolling Stone magazine review was absolutely first class and praised the band no end. Ruben then played the ace. Chives produced a photograph of himself as a kitten stood in a poverty stricken burrow in Weaselville and the front cover of the album was changed to show the photograph. The British press then changed its tune and backed Chives and his band. *Weaselville* was a total success on both sides of the Atlantic. The band then prepared for their gig in Central Park.

The Central Park Free Concert

With the success of the album Chives and Ruben decided to hold a free concert in Central Park, New York City for all the creatures in the area. Several of the New York yards were to organise the security. Word traveled fast around the state and nearly a million creatures turned up to watch the band. It was the biggest musical success the city had ever seen. Chives and his band saw the rebellion out in America as heroes of peace.

Chapter 7

The Yards

Every port city in England has a yard that is run by weasels. In a lot of respects the creatures that live and work in these places are very much on the fringe of woodland society. However, in comment about themselves and their way of life they see themselves very much as the main event of all things furry. In 1964 the yards were the only places where weasels and stoats worked and lived side by side so it is not surprising that they only joined in with any actions of the rebellion after the relief of Weaselvillle in 1966. The three main establishments at this period were Mingo's Yard in Bristol in the southwest, Harry The Juice's Yard at Bethnal Green in the east end of London and Tatlock's Yard on Salford Quays in Manchester. Bristol and London being weasel controlled and Manchester stoat controlled. Even during the heaviest fighting stoats and weasels worked and lived together in the yards without compromise.

During the siege of Weaselville, which is some way from the major cities, a stoat kitten died of malnutrition in a bankrupt southern woodland orphanage. Harry the Juice and Mingo Waterwell bank rolled the orphanage and then took the kitten's body by cart through the SRA lines surrounding Weaselville. Legend has it that the SRA commander who greeted them kissed their paws and bowed before them but in reality Harry and Mingo were questioned for two hours before being allowed through. On arrival at General Acorn's headquarters at Flax Bourton Airfield, Mingo pulled back the tarpaulin on the cart to reveal the kitten's body and said to Acorn that the kitten's death was his responsibility and asked why Woodland Government was only concerned with fighting when the rest of the woodland population were starving to death after the old government had fallen.

Acorn after deliberation called a meeting with the southern scrap yard owners. A plan was drawn up that both yards that were controlled by weasels in the south would open their gates and accept war widows and their kittens from weasel, stoat and vole backgrounds, as well as the poor. In return they would get a reprieve from all accusations, pending prosecutions and prosecutions of anything connected with any form of woodland crime, which also included smuggling. Both Mingo and Harry knew that they would also have to send their finest (their sons) to join the WCGA. Mingo's adoptive son Morteki Ben Adam Brock (Brocky the Weasel) and Harry's son Dave Juice: Brocky to go to the 5th Airborne Section 22 and Dave Juice to the East London Scratchers. Tatlock's Yard in Manchester also saw the entrance of Vince Tatlock to the Stoat Rebel Army after word had got out about the southern yards. As soon as this happened the Woodland Army posted a team of medics and hospital tents to to each yard.

September 1st 1966

The gates of the southern yards opened to the public. Verli the Vole tells her story.

"After my husband's death at the relief of Weaselville I thought life was over. I was left destitute with two kittens to feed. Things were going from bad to worse for us and I couldn't seem to make ends meet at all. The was a story going around that there was to be some form of help coming from General Acorn for mothers and kittens that lived in the cities. This help came for us in the shape of Mingo's Yard. I was told by a neighbour that the yard, that was on the banks of the Cut in Bristol, was opening its gates and accepting mothers with kittens from all backgrounds and they were providing food, shelter and medical care. Many of the vole mothers and widows wouldn't go to Mingo's as they said it was immoral there and that their kittens once in there would never come out the same as they went in. They would become criminals. In my heart I knew there would be a chance of this if we went there to live but in real practicalities I knew that it may not be true and we would die if we didn't go there sooner or later. Creatures were dying everywhere in the cities and the countryside had DDT sprayed all over it.

So I took the plunge to take myself and my kittens to the dreaded and feared Mingo's Yard. There were all sorts of stories about this place; the gangland atmosphere, the hard nutted foreman Brocky and last but not least the ever benevolent Mingo whose orders would be followed not matter what. On arrival I joined the queue of weasel and stoat females stretching down the street. I was the only vole there. As I rounded the corner I could see army medics rushing into the queue with stretchers to pick up females and kittens who had fainted through what looked like malnutrition and further down was stood a WCGA army nurse in a starched white uniform. Finally I got to the gates of the yard. Mingo Waterwell, who was wearing a bus company over coat and medals, looked at me then at my husband's army pay book that had Section 22 Henley-on-Thames Light Cavalry stamped on it, tipped his trilby hat at me then waved me in. This is where I first met Brocky the Weasel. Brocky stood in front of me looking at me in absolute contempt. He was obviously on leave and was wearing fatigue trousers and a Hawaiian shirt. The fur on his head was in the style of a teddy boy. His mouth opened and he uttered the words "You're lucky to be here". Brocky hadn't noticed my husband's pay book so I just looked away and carried on walking with my two kittens.

I couldn't help noticing as I walked through the yard that there was no inner sanctum as the press had reported some years earlier and where were the skulls on sticks that everyone talked about? There were a lot of cars stacked on top of one another and lots of engines stacked high in the air. I found the place where we were going to live which was a corner of a hut marked "females for duration" and started to make up our beds. All of a sudden there was a knock on the door. As I looked there was Brocky standing there. He was waving to my kittens so I headed towards him. My heart skipped a beat as he brought out a flick knife in front of us and said "Your father was killed by them and I will kill them with this". He then bowed in front of us and gave my kittens an SRA cap badge each, claiming that he had personally killed the two stoats who wore them. There was a hint of bravado in Brocky's voice and a later inspection of the cap badges showed they had never been worn and were from some SRA store that had been overrun. It seemed that Mingo's Yard were big on image, bravado and manners. We spent the next eleven years at Mingo's Yard, my kittens never suffered and in some ways were better off for the experience. Mingo Waterwell, his wife and staff ran a tight ship, but a fair one also, and we were all looked after"

By the end of that year word had gone around the yards of southern England that weasel spiritual leader Lemon Grass was coming to the country to visit all creatures involved in the rebellion and that he would be visiting the yards. Lemon Grass was the eternal refugee and a thorn in the side of the old woodland government as cult followings were not their scene at all. He spent his early years in one of the Armenian enclaves but was very much a borderless character. He was followed by millions of creatures all over western Europe. In 1936 he was imprisoned by the Nazis for his indigenous life style and then escaped with the Woodland Free French army at Dunkirk in 1940. On arrival in the United Kingdom he was celebrated by the British. Churchill knew that with Lemon Grass on his side this would secure a free woodland following of the allied forces. The yards in 1966 were more than ready to receive Lemon Grass as they were now involved in one of the biggest social upheavals that the woodland had ever seen.

In February 1967 Lemon Grass arrived at Mingo's Yard with his usual ceremony of bugles and drums. A signal was sent that day direct from General Acorn's headquarters, which were now at Edgebaston in Birmingham, to the WCGA medics at the yard. Acorn and his government had welcomed the cult leader with open arms. This put the seal on making the rebellion very much a creatures' war in both Acorn and the woodland public's eye. The 1967 Lemon Grass tour was a success and he was welcomed both in the south and by the stoats in the North. The yards were now on the side of their respective leaders and an all out guerrilla war was approaching in the North. Still to this day woodland intellectuals argue about whether the yards joined the rebellion as benevolent creatures or did they join it to show how powerful they were, with a mysterious cult figure at the head of their armies who partied with both sides?

Chapter 8

Northumberland, 1967 - 1977

By December 1967 a front line that stretched from Aberystwyth to Great Yarmouth was set up by the Woodland Central Government Army. General Acorn and his staff had also set up their headquarters at Edgebaston in Birmingham. Wales was a woodland free state and all front line duties were monitored by the Free Welsh Woodland Army. In saying this though, John Jones' Yard in Cardiff opened their gates to all creatures in 1967 in line with the English yards. As the year wore on human DDT drops became less and less and the woodland started to recover. From Birmingham to the Isle of Seals (Isle of Wight) weasels and voles were joining the WCGA. More and more training camps were opening and section 22 was filling its ranks with recruits from the yards. The new front was to be in the North East. Arthur Jenkins' army had recovered from its withdrawal, had regrouped and were preparing to fight in their own open country. Section 22 training was tough, it had to be - the recruits from the yards were hard core creatures who found it hard to accept military discipline. The hoop was in place but this was water off a duck's back to many of the recruits. It was decided that for one group of recruits, with Brocky the Weasel in its ranks, Sergeant Jebediah Honeycut was to be brought in. Honeycut had all the makings of an airborne weasel and was from a similar background to many of the section 22 recruits. Brocky's section was a strange one - it was made up of a cross section of woodland life and embodied all the strengths and weaknesses of this part of the Woodland Army. However within three months C Section, B Coy, 5th Airborne Regiment were ready to go into action in Northumberland.

The nominal roll for C Section, B Coy, 5th Airborne Regiment, Section 22, Woodland Central Government Army, Acorn Barracks, Shepton Mallet, Somerset, November 1967

40006734 Sergeant, Honeycut, J, Weasel, Regular Army

40855889, Cpl, McGraph, B, Weasel, Regular Army

40085567, L/ Cpl, Eccles, J, Vole, Henley-on-Thames Light Cavalry, Medic

40084588, L/ Cpl, Ticklefish, J, Vole, Henley-on-Thames Light Cavalry,
Radio Operator

40789775, Pte Fleetwood, G, Weasel, Rifle-creature

40083589 Pte Brock M, B, A, Weasel, Rifle-creature

40863890, Pte Harcourt, R, J, Weasel, Rifle-creature

In March 1968 intelligence reports from members of the HOTLC that were dug in, in Northumberland told of large numbers of stoats bringing in supplies of weapons and ammunition from the Bolton area. The whole of the SRA in the North East were being re-armed and re-supplied. However their troops were not being deployed in large numbers. They were occupying stoat villages and stream areas. This led to Acorn deciding that the best way of fighting the SRA for the WCGA would be on their paws by sending in the airborne to assess and evaluate situation, then deploy the ground troops and artillery support. At the end of March the first airborne drop was made over the Cheviots by one company of 4th Airborne WCGA. Their orders were to march the area and send back intelligence reports. As soon as they landed they were shot to pieces. They never made their objective and were captured by The Liverpool and Merseyside Free Stoats who were on covert operations in that area. It was decided that all direct drops were to be cancelled in the future and that the Cheviots were to be won inch by inch. The next drop was by the 5th and 6th Airborne regiments. This meant that Brocky and Jervaise Ticklefish, after all the deliberation, agreements and social upheaval, were going into action. By now the voles from the Woodland Air Force had dropped their defunct battle dress jackets and detachable collars and were wearing airborne smocks and Hawaiian shirts with all their flying accoutrements. Voles were cool creatures and they fought the rebellion their way. In April 20 DC1 aircraft took off from Flax Bourton Airfield for the drop on Wooler, which was a purist stoat town, but lightly defended. Intelligence reports were correct and Wooler was taken in a matter of hours. Although the fighting was heavy the small unit of Middlesbrough 56 were outgunned and had taken a battering by the WCGA airborne artillery before they surrendered.

Wooler, The gateway to the Cheviots

Once Wooler was taken, Acorn conducted further drops and opened a corridor to the south bringing in the ground forces. Beyond Wooler, though, was the whole of the SRA with dug in pivot guns and booby traps laid everywhere.

The fighting in the four hundred and five square miles of Northumberland saw some of the most controversial and fierce actions of the WCGA during the rebellion. The following stories are told in the troopers' own words.

L/ Cpl, Jervaise Tickelfish, vole, Henley-on-Thames Light Cavalry, radio operator

"I had only ever been to the North once before which was for a woodland poetry competition when I was a student in 1964. The landscape there was very like something from the famous woodland novel The Catcher In My Pie which was about a stoat who educated himself and went on a journey of spiritual enlightenment. As soon as I jumped from the aircraft I could see the land below. The view was tremendous. Wooler appeared to be an endless series of hills with the Cheviot being the highest. As soon as we landed all aspects of enjoying the view ended and we fought the battle of Wooler. The SRA were dug in with pivot guns but other than this they were thin on the ground. Myself and my section dodged the rounds by hiding behind human buildings and all ran into a tea shop seeking shelter to the amazement of the human population. I can recall that Brocky and co. liberated one or two cakes from this establishment during the fight, as well as the till, according to our company

commander some time later. The fighting went on for some time and was fierce but we all survived it. There were further drops and more troops brought in as the 4th Airborne opened the corridor to the south.

Wooler soon became the main supply depot for all operations in Northumberland for the next nine years. After the battle we were stood down and had to share the town with a very uneasy stoat civilian population who thought we were going to kill them. However after a while we enjoyed better relations with them until we left for Yeavering Bell hill fort. This was an objective given to us to secure further ground and ultimately win the rebellion. The march to the hill fort was a terrible one thwart with booby traps and fire fights with small sections of the SRA. It was on this march that we lost Private Rixie Harcourt. Rixie was just your average goons in lots of ways - he had spent some time in HMWP Swindon but other than that lived a quiet life. On a day when the wind and rain was driving down he stepped on an SRA booby trap. These devices were crude affairs, usually a human banger in a paint can that was spring loaded. It was awful. I heard a thud some way behind me and then a scream. When I got back to Rixie he was lying on the ground, bleeding to death with his paws blown off. The medic, Eccles, was doing what he could but Rixie died in his arms. We buried Rixie fifteen miles outside Wooler in the worst weather that I had ever seen. After this the whole section went silent for days until we reached a stoat village some miles on.

The stoats in this part of world didn't have much to do with weasels and voles, they lived as they had always lived and in some respects knew nothing of the rebellion. Most of the SRA were from the big cities of the North. The local creatures weren't the politicals of Salford 101. We searched each burrow for anything suspicious and found nothing except terrified stoat families who were crying and bowing in front of us. All of a sudden Goff Fleetwood seemed to go mad as he tore an innocent stoat's burrow to pieces and shot everything in sight. He then grabbed the head of the stoat family and dragged him to a tree where a rope was being thrown over in the shape of a hangman's noose. The stoats were begging them to stop but things were escalating - this was a reprisal for Rixie's death. I ran to our sergeant and pointed out what was about to happen. He ran over, recited some deep verse from the book of Pan and the potential atrocity was stopped. The effect this had on the stoats was awful. They were now in absolute fear of us and word traveled fast through the Cheviot Hills. I knew from this point on I would be in an all out conflict with no boundaries or winners, just massacre, carnage and sorrow for the stoats caught up in the wider scheme of things. Goff Fleetwood with given two weeks Regimental Prison and a month's loss of pay for his actions"

L/ Cpl, Julius Eccles, vole, Henley-on-Thames Light Cavalry, medic

"After what became known as the Northumberland Incident we marched on Yeavering Bell hill fort. Our intelligence reports from The City of Westminster Vole Regiment showed that we were going up against the politicals of Salford 101. This would mean heavy casualties and a fight to the death. There would be no prisoners in this fight either way, and now that Stoat Free Radio in Manchester had got hold of what they called an atrocity, we would be fighting for our lives and not just a very southern cause of who's the best at drawing and painting. We got to about half a mile from the hill and then dug in. From what we could see our own artillery were being used against us. Salford 101 had captured one of our batteries and we could see flaming coals being fired from the top of the hill falling just short of our position. Once the barrage stopped we then attacked the hill. It was a slaughter – we were cut down where we stood. This is where Jervaise Ticklefish was wounded. Jervaise took a hot round straight in his back and went down on the ground. I ran over to him and turned him over. He was still conscious so I applied a plasma drip to him and bandaged his wounds. Jervaise then regained full consciousness and sat up. At this point we were ordered to withdraw from the hill so I shouted for two stretcher bearers who then took him to the rear of our position.

We were near completely surrounded with Salford 101 still firing at us and they had now brought up a pivot gun as well. The whole company was withdrawn even further back, away from the stoat artillery. We couldn't move Jervaise and had to leave to him to the mercy of the advancing SRA. We offered him five hundred rounds of ammunition and rations but all he asked for was my copy of the Bhagavad Gita. Once this was in his paw he looked towards the sky ignoring the battle and said "Vishnu, I have become death, the destroyer of worlds". I told him that this was no time for blasphemy. He said he wasn't committing blasphemy and was in regret for taking up the sword and not starving to death in Henley and keeping his higher self. After this we left to the sound of hordes of stoats coming down the hill. Jervaise was picked up by Tyne and Wear 42 who treated him as an enemy, but were gracious towards him. He was sent by steam train to the Stoat Rebel Army Medical Service, 48 Regiment General Hospital at Bolton where he delivered his famous sonnet about peace in the woodland whilst being interviewed by the SRA Military Police. Jervaise Ticklefish is now head of Southbank Woodland Arts in London".

I would like to step in whilst writing this book and say that the next interview was a difficult one to obtain. I wrote to Mingo Waterwell and didn't receive a reply for over six months. My reply came from James McGraph, a vole employed as the yard clerk. I was invited for a meeting with Morteki Ben Adam Brock at Canadian Jack's Cafe and Grill Bar, which is situated between Mingo's Yard and Bernie Eccles' International Boxing Gymnasium, on the banks of the cut near Dean Lane in Bristol. As I entered the cafe I saw Brocky sat with what could only be described as a motley crew. He was dressed in a boiler suit and donkey jacket with a quiff in the fur on his head. He and his friends were playing a card game that I didn't understand called Chase the Ace. Brocky's eye caught me and he spoke to me in broad Bristolian *"Sit down scribe and I will be with you in a minute"* he said. Brocky had the winning paw and played on. Once he had collected his winnings he then gestured to me and the barman to go to a back room where he offered me a seat. Once the drinks had arrived Brocky looked me straight in the eye and didn't back up. He then pulled what looked like a flick knife from his pocket, pointed it at me, then pressed the catch and out of the case came a comb with which he adjusted his quiff. *"Put you in your place there, vole"* he laughingly said out loud. I knew now that the formalities were over, that Brocky the Weasel was ready to talk. His story is as follows:

Pte Mortekai Ben Adam Brock, Rifle-creature, weasel, B Coy 5th Airborne WCGA.

"I was dropped into Northumberland with B Coy 5th Airborne. To us we were the complete works even though there were voles with us. We took and held the town of Wooler whilst all the crap hats came up to meet us. Got to say it, we had a rye old time in Wooler, there were one or two weasel females that were glad to see us there and to be honest with you all the civvie stoats were hiding. Well let's face it an amateur army like that should of fucked off as soon as we arrived and not even bothered to fight us.

We only had to withdraw at Yeavering Bell hill fort because the crap hats got bogged down at the rear. In my view the Stoat Rebel Army as they called themselves were a shower of shit that couldn't fight their way out of a paper bag. The stoats that we had at the yard then and now are of a different kind and are more like us but I am not going be politically correct about these fuckers whatsoever. Fuck em then and fuck em now. There's also a lot of talk that I killed the Rat of Tangiers in Northumberland. As I sit here and as Pan is my witness my company wasn't in the area that day. The Woodland Army has confirmed this on tv. I fought all the other battles in that area and was

demobbed at Birmingham in 1977 where I got back to the yard and became foreman. Lets face it vole, what did we get out of the rebellion? Nothing! Its the stoats and the voles that hold all the cards these days. This business also about our immunity from prosecution that was given to us by Acorn, we don't commit crime at the yards and never have done".

All three stories show that the fight in Northumberland wasn't a walk over as the woodland press would have suggested at that period. They tell of heroism, compassion by both sides and a lot of pride and guts. After the withdrawal from the hill fort the 1973 peace talks were only around the corner.

The 1973 Peace Talks

In mid 1973 stalemate set in and each side had its position in Northumberland from the previous years of fighting. The peace talks were to be held at Blackpool in Lancashire and would be attended by the spiritual leader Lemon Grass (whose idea it was), human leader Edward Heath, General Acorn and Arthur Jenkins. The sight that greeted the human holiday makers at Blackpool would have been a sight to see. The whole event was to be organised and managed by the City of Westminster Vole Regiment who were busy from April onwards carrying inks, quills and parchments (whilst dressed in their no.1 uniform, shirt, tie and slouch hat) in and out of the ballroom at Blackpool Tower which also had the WCGA Military Police checking the passes of those who entered and left the building . The surrounding area to the beach was cordoned off by barbed wire. The date was set for the 30th May when all leaders met.

The record of the talks are as follows:

**Woodland Central Government Army and Stoat Rebel Army Peace
Talks, Blackpool Tower, Blackpool, Lancashire,
May 30th – June 1st 1973**

Attendees:

The honourable and respected Lemon Grass; General Acorn, Officer Commanding The Woodland Central Government Army; Arthur Jenkins, Officer Commanding The Stoat Rebel Army; Edward Heath, Human Leader.

Motions carried:

1. All DDT attacks by humans on the woodland population to cease by 0600hrs, June 1st

2. All attacks by the human navy to cease on all weasel privateer boats by 0600 hrs. June 1st

3. All searches and pursuits of weasel privateer boats to be carried out by the RWN.

4. All contraband to be retained by crews for private sale and profit if privateer boats can out run the RWN craft.

5. Mink, Captain Deville to be released from HMWP Swindon and compensated for the sinking of the privateer the *Pride of The Frome* in the mouth of the Severn estuary in 1962.

6. WCGA airborne to be issued Hard Tack Biscuits and Strawberry Jam as rations, Henley-on-Thames Light Cavalry to be issued with Rich Tea Biscuits and Apricot Jam as rations from 0600hrs June 1st

7. All regiments of the Stoat Rebel Army to be issued with Bread and Dripping as rations every other Monday from 0600hrs June 1st.

8. Mingo Waterwell, Harry The Juice and Vince Tatlock to be given sole rights to docking, loading and unloading at their respective rivers and establishments.

The peace talks were a bold initiative by Lemon Grass but in the cause of peace they failed and after an uneasy two day cease fire both sides went back into conflict. The agreement records clearly show that the yards came out of the talks well and landed on their paws.

The Rat of Tangiers.

In mid 1974 the Stoat Rebel Army army entered what could be viewed as an unattractive period. They were losing minor battles and the army in general was not performing as well as it had in previous years. This was blamed on the bread and dripping at first but this was later disproved. Because of this Arthur Jenkins decided upon a visit to North Africa. This was where he would make contact with the Rat of Tangiers and his four thousand strong merce-nary group. These soldiers of fortune were mostly rats but also a mish-mash of creatures from all over the furry world. In August the first soldiers started to arrive in the stoat lines. They were hard fighters and had their own fully automatic weapons and an endless supply of ammunition.

The first that the WCGA knew about this was when a company of the 6th Airborne attacked Hedge Hope Hill where they were faced with rats, heavily armed with automatic weapons, who were coming at them from all sides. The 6th had to withdraw and the psychological effect on them was a heavy one. When WCGA command received the news they told their troops to ignore the mercenaries and fight on. There were only four thousand of them and their pay in the end may bankrupt Arthur Jenkins. The biggest problem the merce-naries posed was that if they fought in the rebellion they would have a claim over the rivers and waterways. The yards on both sides were counting on the fact that no matter who won the rebellion things would more or less stay the same, however, with a large number rats claiming a possible victory their power may shift and they would lose their grip. Unknown to the yards at this time was the fact that the rebellion itself was creating a huge social change in the woodland and things would never be the same again once it was over. A meeting was called, well away from the sight of the commanders of both armies. Mingo Waterwell, Harry The Juice and a representative from Tat-lock's Yard met in Worcestershire to seal the fate of rats. It was decided that either Brocky the Weasel or Vince Tatlock would fight the Rat of Tangiers to the death. It all depended on who was in the area nearest to the rat who would take part in the fight. If Brocky or Vince won then things stayed the same - if they didn't all hell would break loose. A war within a war would start, with parts of both sides fighting as one group. It was also decided that the SRA would deliver the Rat of Tangiers, at his agreement, to the WCGA lines.

Fate dealt a paw that Brocky was in the nearest area.

The following account is by:

Private J. Berryman, radio operator, vole, The City of Westminster Vole Regiment.

"The airborne were short of radio operators so I was posted to the B Coy 5th Airborne. This was a Section 22 unit who did things a lot differently to what I was used to in my own regiment. In some ways this was the sharp end and it could be very vicious in and out of the fighting. On the morning of September

1st I woke and prepared myself for the day. Around mid morning all of our senior ranks seemed to disappear. I was then ordered by my superior to grab my radio and tune into a Stoat Rebel Army frequency. This was an offence with a heavy penalty where I had come from and I hesitated at the order. My superior just looked at me and told me to carry on. I tuned into the frequency and could hear an SRA unit trying to make contact with me. I answered their message and they replied by giving me a grid reference about ten minutes walk from where we were. We arrived at the grid reference and were greeted by the strangest sight I had seen during the rebellion. There was the Stoat Rebel Army almost face to face with us. They had bolt action rifles and what looked like a World War II radio which sat awkwardly on their signaler's back. They spoke the same language but couldn't look us in the eye. All I could see was their caps that had Che Guevara badges sewn on them. Behind them stood a very large rat who wore an open fatigue shirt with a Satanic symbol hanging around his neck. In his belt was tucked a jewel encrusted Moroccan dagger. Both sides said nothing then all of a sudden I felt a tap on my shoulder: it was Brocky. He looked at me and said "Turn that wireless off". I then knew what was going to happen. Brocky was going to fight the Rat of Tangiers to the death. I was horrified, this wasn't what the army or the rebellion was about - this was criminality in its true essence and I was in the middle of it. There was nothing that I could do so I stayed silent.

Brocky walked towards the Rat and the two started to wrestle, Brocky went down and the Rat seemed to get the better of him. Then the two got up, still locked together. A weird thing then happened, a bird made a noise which seemed to startle the Rat, who fell backwards then righted himself. He then pulled the dagger from his belt. At this point I thought Brocky was going to be murdered but things changed and Brocky brought up his paw and kicked dust in the eyes of the Rat who dropped the dagger on the floor. Brocky picked up the dagger and stabbed the Rat of Tangiers straight through the chest with it and killed him. The Rat died screaming in a pool of blood on the floor. Legend has it that Brocky recited an ancient verse over his body, but he said nothing and just walked away. It was awful"

The Woodland Army still deny that the 5th Airborne were in the part of Cheviots where a mercenary's body was found that had been killed with a sacrificial dagger. Both sides still maintain that no mercenaries were used by any army between 1965 and 1977 in any theatre of hostilities during the civil war.

1975–1977

1975 saw the nearing of the end of the rebellion. The SRA were suffering intermittent deliveries of their ammunition from North Africa and most of their mercenaries had left for home or other wars that no one cares to write about. By 1976 the SRA had lost the Cheviot to the WCGA and only had control of Hedge Hope Hill. Arthur Jenkins decided to withdraw most of his troops back to the Rotherham area whilst sending the Yorkshire and Lancashire Scratchers to defend 48 Regiment General Hospital which was at Bolton. In January 1976 small skirmish style fighting was still going on in the Cheviots. The Northumberland Stoat Brigade were the last to leave along with 402 Pivot Gun Field Regiment. The whole of this year saw a rear guard action in Northumberland by the SRA and their total withdrawal from the area. In January 1977 the WCGA were advancing towards Rotherham and Bolton.

Chapter 9

Capitulation

In 1976 the rebellion was winding down. One of the biggest factors of this was that the SRA were running out of ammunition. After the use of mercenaries their funds were down and they were almost bankrupt. The Northumberland Stoat Brigade were the only creatures of the SRA that were left in the Cheviots. The WCGA had taken nearly all the ground in this region. Arthur Jenkins and most of the SRA were now at Rotherham and Bolton. The WCGA knew that the oncoming victory would be a difficult one both before and after the fighting had finished.

In June of that year after a fierce fire fight the Northumberland Stoat Brigade and 402 Pivot Gun Field Regiment surrendered to the 5th Airborne WCGA. Most of the fighting in the Cheviots had now ceased and the push towards Rotherham and Bolton was about to begin. The SRA were regrouping around these towns with Salford 101 putting up a heavy rear guard who were ready to defend them to the death. Acorn then withdrew the 5th Airborne and dropped in the 4th and 6th along with The Gloucester Weasel Brigade, The East Anglian Berry Pickers, The Medway Voles, 384 Catapult Field Regiment and 307 Catapult Airborne Regiment inclusive of the Henley-on-Thames Light Cavalry to flush out the crack SRA rear guard. Gradually Salford 101 withdrew south to Rotherham. The journey that the SRA made was a perilous one where all their wounded had to be taken by goat drawn cart. The crossing of the Peak District lost some fifty thousand stoats who had to be buried along the road side. Out of nearly seven hundred and fifty thousand stoats who fought the battles of the Cheviots only seven hundred thousand made it back to Rotherham and then for the lucky few a hospital bed at Bolton. By this time the WCGA were advancing south faster than their supplies could reach them and they came to a halt at the edge of the Peak District. This created a window where the SRA finally withdrew its remaining soldiers to the safety of Yorkshire. Aircraft were dispatched from Somerset and made drop after drop of supplies. After a few months the WCGA were on the move again. The airborne had been regrouped and were ready to drop on both Bolton and Rotherham. The ground forces would then split in two to take both towns.

On the February 2nd 1977 the 5th Airborne WCGA dropped ten miles outside Rotherham. They met light resistance: the blood bath that was expected had not happened. Unknown to them the whole of the SRA had now ran out of ammunition and medical supplies. The ground forces quickly came up to meet them. The same happened at Bolton. On February 4th a cease fire was declared and the 5th Airborne were withdrawn with the Home Counties Regiment inclusive of the Knightsbridge and Chelsea Voles Territorial Brigade being brought up to replace them. This move on Acorn's part was due to the fact that a line regiment was a better choice to handle what could be a surrender than a hard core section 22 airborne unit. The City of Westminster Vole Regiment were sent to Bolton for the same duties. By 1400hrs of that day Arthur Jenkins had surrendered to the Writers and Dandies of London. After twelve years the fighting was over.

Surrender

At 1500hrs on February 5th 1977 General Acorn of the Woodland Central Government Army met with Arthur Jenkins of the Stoat Rebel Army at Rotherham Town Hall. Arthur Jenkins, in the presence of six bowler hatted voles from Woodland Central Government, signed the unconditional surrender of the Stoat Rebel Army. All regiments of the SRA received the radio message, *a bunch of primroses* at 1505 hrs this was the code word for capitulation.

Arthur Jenkins final speech to the English Stoat Nation at 1500hrs, February 5th, 1977 Rotherham, South Yorkshire

"Comrades we have struggled together and we have fought bravely, our equality will never be taken from us: all of those cornfields and ballet in the evening will live in our hearts for ever"

Birmingham and the road home

After the surrender the SRA were regrouped, disarmed and placed into captivity awaiting transportation to the south of England for confinement and eventual demobilisation. Within one month the woodland railways were back open and both the WCGA who weren't on peace keeping duties and captured SRA were going to be transported to Birmingham which would become the hub of all military dispersals over the next seven months. Over one million creatures had to be processed. The human local councils at Rotherham, Bolton and Birmingham agreed to close parts of their city and town centres also their railway stations to the public to let the soldiers leave. The scenes at Bolton and Rotherham were ones of organised chaos. Thousands of troops were moving through the town centres. There were captured stoats under guard with weasels and voles making their way to the railway stations still in their regiments. Hundreds of carts and goats had to be loaded for flat back rail transportation. Captured SRA transport was either disabled or taken to be reused by the WCGA. 48 Regiment General Hospital at Bolton who were now under the command of the WCGA were dealing with the wounded from both armies.

The end of the rebellion saw its human recognition. As the first train from Rotherham reached Birmingham both human and woodland aid charities came to meet it. The RSPCA, PDSA, National Weasel Centres and Saint Tickle's were on the platform to meet the SRA and WCGA. Tents were set up in the city centre and Birmingham bus station was turned into a temporary camp. Captured SRA were held behind barbed wire in tented accommodation about five hundred yards from the bus station. The mayor decreed that because of the situation all bookmakers and bars were allowed to stay open for twenty four hours a day on one condition; that the beaten and now demoralised Stoat Rebel Army were given partial freedom. General Acorn during a meeting with the mayor at his headquarters in Edgebaston only agreed to this as long as they had the letters POW clearly marked on their back and there were designated bars and bookmakers for them to visit. This agreement worked and the stoats were given partial freedom. By late August demobilisation of the WCGA was well on its way. A new army was going to be set up which would be renamed the Woodland Democratic Army. The rebellion had many effects one of which was the fact that the SRA, even though it has lost the war, had raised an awareness to all creatures that the woodland would not be able to carry on in the way that it had. No one wanted this to happen again.

For the creatures of the Southwest the general route home was from New Street Station by train to Cardiff then a trip across the Severn by boat to Portishead dock in North Somerset. The scene at New Street was a very busy one with walking wounded being helped on to the train and POW's who were off to be demobbed in Somerset boarding under armed guard. Brocky the Weasel came back this way and then caught the train back to Bristol where he was greeted at the yard by Mingo and all creatures that lived there. Mingo wore his medals for Brocky's return and an old faded union jack was hung up. All of the sights on New Street station the most endearing was the sight and sound of a creature playing the Yelk. These instruments were carried mainly by stoats attached to their back packs through all the battles of the rebellion. Northumberland saw its greatest use during the stalemate. The Yelk's roots go back to prehistoric times and an expert stoat, weasel or vole can play sophisticated melodies that out class any human instrument.

By November 1977 a new woodland government had been created with the full inclusion of stoats, who now enjoyed full equality in any job they chose to do. Woodland mainstream and fringe arts are now run by voles. Although the élite still hold their arts competitions it is only they who enter them and win them whereas the rest of woodland now run the arts between them. The Yelk, which was only played by the fringe, has now become a recognised instrument and its music takes to the international stage.

The Woodland is now a far better place than it was before 1965. Stoats, weasels and voles now exist in harmony. General Acorn, who stood shoulder to shoulder with his fellow creatures, became the head of the Woodland Democratic Government in 1977. He then closed the Sai Jean hostess bar in Weaselville and allowed stoats to keep the names of their regiments when the WDA was formed. This led to an attempt on his life by a fringe group of demobbed WCGA airborne soldiers, that when captured said that "no woodland soldier would ever raise his rifle against them". They were executed by firing squad in 1979. This was dramatised in the 1982 film "The Day of The Weasel". General Acorn is now head of English Woodland Land Forces. Arthur Jenkins was placed in confinement at the end of the rebellion and then released in 1980. He is now the chair of the Woodland Council of the North of England.

The Stoat rebellion could be viewed in many ways and woodland historians have argued many times over why it was fought. But during the writing of this book I felt that it had raised questions for me. One of my questions was this, no one can doubt that the yards were benevolent towards all creatures during the rebellion. However, did they also use the conflict to show how powerful they were? The Blackpool peace talks ended with the yards coming out on top and a return to hostilities.

Morteki Brock, Dave Juice and Vince Tatlock wouldn't have starved during the rebellion, no one in the yards ever did, before or after the relief of Weaseville. They joined their armies because they were told to do by their bosses. This book dedicates Donovan's song *Universal Soldier* to them.

Appendix

I never knew the old Weaselville before the Rebellion with its classical music, its glamour and easy charm; West London suited me better. I really got to know it in the classic period of the devil-may-care east part of the city. Back in those days some would say that you hadn't had a night out in the city unless you had been thrown out of the doors of the Sai Jean by the airborne on a Saturday night.

In 1965 I found myself sitting in a deserted WBC television studio at Teddington Lock. The élite had left for the collective farms. Whilst sat alone amongst the lifeless equipment with thoughts of starvation I had an idea. Why not ask the WCGA to commandeer the equipment and create a new television station? I had served in the airborne myself at Arnhem in World War II and knew that General Acorn would give me five minutes at the least. I contacted him and he agreed to a meeting. I wore my black bowler hat and was accompanied by my old black umbrella when I met Acorn. He told me in no uncertain terms that my idea was a very fine one but there were strings attached if he was going to agree to it. There would be payment, but only a small retainer, plus rations for each creature that worked for me; that all broadcasts other than the daily news had to include light entertainment for his army; Peyton Place and the Fosdyke Saga had to go and would be replaced by Top of the Pops and the Golden Shot. I said this was not a problem as the human networks would sell us what we wanted at a favourable rate even though the DDT crisis was unfolding. We managed to get many a Sunday night drama, and Open University programme for vole regiments, at a knock down price. I knew this was going to be a creatures' war so I was fully prepared. In March 1965 we recruited our first workers, mainly voles, graduates that had been left to starve, but also some weasels. By December we had made out first broadcast. WITV was born.

During the Siege of Weaselville we broadcast live from the Sai Jean as the city held its breath during the last days before the first victory. Before and after the relief we embedded our crews with various units of the WCGA also. This worked exceedingly well and after a very short while we had the common soldier on our side and we reciprocated. The Stoat Rebel Army did accuse us of misreporting and bias, however we didn't see it like that. We did approach Arthur Jenkins for permission to interview and film his troops in 1974 but he refused. The fight in Northumberland was a long and arduous one that sadly saw twelve members of our embedded crews killed in action. However, on the up side of the fight in the North, after the 1973 peace talks saw the introduction of advertising into our schedule, our commercials became the marching songs of the WCGA. Advertising also made us independently funded and after the rebellion had finished this was a licence to print money. Woodland Independent Television still runs and is the most watched station by creatures like yourselves in Britain today.

Sir Mungo Robinson, Vole, Head of Woodland Independent Television

Glossary

AD: Air defence, defence of the ground from air attack. The original Pivot Gun took the form of a wheeled gun with one barrel, an optical tracker unit, a generator and trailer of stores. The whole system, along with the crew, was delivered by a goat drawn cart. Later versions had two barrels. The pivot gun was originally designed as a field gun but its high elevation gave it the dual role as a highly accurate air defence weapon. It is still in service with the WDA. Between 1965 – 1977 four hundred and twenty five aircraft of the WAF were shot down by 408 Pivot Gun Air Defence Regiment of the Stoat Rebel Army.

Airborne: Airborne forces are woodland military units (infantry and artillery) that are set up to be moved by aircraft and 'dropped' into battle. Thus they can be placed behind enemy lines, and have an ability to deploy almost anywhere with little warning. The formations are limited only by the number and size of their aircraft, so given enough capacity a huge force can appear "out of nowhere" in minutes: an action referred to as vertical envelopment. Conversely, woodland airborne forces typically lack the supplies and equipment for prolonged combat operations, and are therefore more suited for airhead operations than for long term occupation. Furthermore, parachute operations are particularly sensitive to adverse weather conditions. Advances in woodland helicopter technology since the rebellion have brought increased flexibility to the scope of airborne operations, and air assaults have largely replaced large scale parachute operations. However, due to the limited range of helicopters and the limited number of troops that can be transported by them, the woodland retains Paratroopers as a valuable strategic asset.

Bhagavad Gita: The Bhagavad Gita is technically part of Book 6 of the Mahabharata, although it is known to be a later accretion to the saga, which stands on its own merits. It is a dialog between the God Krishna and the hero Arjuna, taking place in a timeless moment on the battlefield before the climactic struggle between good and evil. The Gita (which can be found in vole burrows throughout the English woodland) is a classic summary of the core beliefs of Hinduism. It has had a significant influence far beyond Hinduism. Jervaise Ticklefish recited the verse from Chapter 11 "Vishnu I have become death, the destroyer of worlds", after being wounded and in regret of his actions.

Brass shoulder titles: Cast brass letters that indicate the regiment of a soldier that are worn on the outer edge of the epaulette of the jacket, e.g. H.O.T.L.C

Collective farms: Organisations where creatures work (growing crops and keeping goats), live and eat together on an equal basis. With ever growing movements for equality in the woodland from the late 1950s onwards, the élite distanced themselves by creating collective farms. These farms were in remote areas and, although their advertising had a welcoming atmosphere, the reality of them was that membership, and even entry at times, was restricted. As the DDT crisis unfolded, the élite retired to their farms, which were in DDT free areas. Many starving weasels and voles turned up at the gates of these establishments but were turned away and left to perish. One of the reasons they were given for this was that their art work and poetry was passé. In reality the collective farms were pseudo-socialist organisations and a front for woodland mainstream arts, where all creatures were equal as long as they were the right creatures.

Composition rations: The Woodland Central Government Army individual combat ration, the CR1C (Combat Ration One Creature), was a complete 24-hour ration pack that provided two substantial meals per day. Most items, such as goon sausage, baked beans, vegetables and chips were contained in tin cans. After the 1973 Peace Talks the WCGA included with every meal pack biscuits, a chocolate bar, coffee, tea, sugar, crackers, cheese spread, jam, sweetened condensed milk, hard sweets, and marmite. The SRA after the 1973 Peace Talks included canned bread and dripping.

Coy: Company

Charging a clip: Placing five rounds, three down two up in a clip that fits into two grooves in the breach of a .101 rifle

Cpl: Corporal (two stripes also known as tapes) rank above Lance Corporal. Any soldier attaining this rank can be in charge of up to six creatures.

Crap hats: Any soldier of the WCGA who was not part of the élite forces of Section 22, who wore red berets. WDA airborne soldiers still use this slang term.

DC1 Aircraft: The Kennington and South London Aircraft Corporation DC1 is a military transport aircraft that was developed from the KSLAC, DC-2 airliner. It was used extensively by the Woodland Central Government Army during the Stoat Rebellion and remained in front line operations throughout the 1980's with a few remaining in operation to this day.

Operational history:

The DC1 was vital to the success of the Woodland Central Government Army's campaigns between 1965 and 1977. They were deployed at the relief of Weaselville and in the Cheviot Hills of Northumberland where the DC1 made it possible for WCGA troops to counter the mobility of the light travelling Stoat Rebel Army. Additionally, DC1s were used to airlift supplies to the embattled ground forces during the battle of Yeavering Bell hill fort. Its most work-a-day role in woodland military aviation was

flying the long haul from Somerset to Northumberland during the rebellion.
Crew: 4 Voles, Pilot, Co Pilot, Navigator and Flight Engineer
Capacity: 98 troopers
Payload: 3,000lb
Length: 32ft 9in
Wingspan: 45ft 6in
Height: 8ft 0in
Wing area: 452ft^2
Empty weight: 9,135lb
Loaded weight: 12,000lb
Max. take off weight: 16,000lb
Powerplant: 2 × Kennington and South London Aircraft Corporation Twin 14-cylinder radial engines, 800hp each

DDT: Dichlorodiphenyltrichloroethane (DDT) is a organochlorine contact insecticide that kills weasels, and voles by acting as a nerve poison. its insecticidal properties were discovered by the Swiss scientist Paul Müller working for J.R. Geigy (now Novartis) in 1942. Exactly how DDT affects a creatures nervous system is not properly understood, although a great deal of work has been done to try and find out its precise mode of action. This Woodland Central Government Army Document (WCGA 5286/A, Restricted) will refer to the technical product 'DDT', which is a mixture of isomers, principally p,p'-DDT, with lesser amounts of o,p'-DDT (isomers are chemicals with the same molecular make-up, but with differing three-dimensional structure). Small amounts of the breakdown products DDD and DDE can also be found in the formulation. DDT was originally used during World War II to control typhus which was spread by the fur louse. Since then it has been used to control mosquito borne malaria, and was used extensively as a general human agricultural insecticide. Initially DDT was spectacularly successful particularly in the control of malaria, as well as against some agricultural pests. But by the late 1950s problems had developed between the human and the woodland government over its use, by 1965, a genocidal crisis had developed between both governments over its use in air burst attacks against creatures in general.

WCGA, Publication 5286/A, Restricted, September 20th 1971

DDT crisis: To deal with the mistake of the introduction of Myxamotosis the human government of the UK sprayed air burst DDT over large areas of the country side. As the crisis unfolded woodland government was stretched to its limit to address the large number of casualties created. Most weasels, stoats and voles lived in areas where the attacks were most prominent. Creatures who lived in the cities were unaffected, but food stocks became low which created a famine for many. A crisis situation was declared by Woodland Central Government in mid 1965 and by the end of that year the high number casualties and deaths were under control. The 1973 Blackpool peace talks saw the end of all air burst DDT attacks on the woodland and it is now banned in the UK.

Goon Fish: Freshly caught Sticklebacks, best served with baked beans and chips, with a light garnish of lemon or mint.

Goon sausage: Goon sausage, both then and now, is the food of the poor. The WCGA and SRA marched on it through the rebellion and it is still served in WDA camps today. The government are trying to ban the use of this food because of its high cholesterol rate, however, the WDA has refused to bargain with them by saying that it would affect recruiting numbers if the ban was enforced. Their most recent comment was that woodland soldiers need to eat what they received in the orphanage or what their mother had cooked them at home to make them feel comfortable. Goon sausage recipe:- flies, spiders and minced goat meat, paw-kneaded together, marinated in brown ale, then lightly fried with olive oil. Best served with baked beans and chips with a light garnish of parsley.

HMWP: Her Majesty's Woodland Prison.

HOTLC: Henley-on-Thames Light Cavalry.

Hot and Cold rounds: Hot rounds were aerodynamically shaped, orange hot coals that were fired from WCGA catapult batteries during the rebellion. The coals were mined in the Forest of Dean and then transported by cart to forward positions on an allocation basis. Cold rounds were very much the same but made from granite.

KSLAC: The Kennington and South London Aircraft Corporation, woodland aircraft manufacturers and flight operators. The company has moved to their new factory and airfield, after eighty years in south London, now just outside Stansted Airport, due to complaints about noise and low flying over the Elephant and Castle.

Line regiment: Any infantry regiment in the WCGA, SRA or WDA that is not part of the élite force.

L/Cpl: Lance Corporal (one stripe, also known as a tape), which is a rank above Private, Gunner (artillery, Lance Bombardier), or Trooper. The rank has its roots in periods when troopers who were senior to infantry privates were taken from the cavalry and placed with the infantry. The cavalry trooper, whilst serving with infantry, would be given the rank of Lance Corporal. Any soldier attaining this rank can be in charge of three or more creatures. During the rebellion it was mainly awarded to voles from the HOTLC who had technical trades.

National Weasel Centres: A woodland charity organisation that has been running for over one hundred years. The NWC, as it is referred to, accepts all creatures and gives care to them when they are on hard times. It also has a youth section. Homelessness, starvation and illness are the major issues in the woodland and the NWC assists with all three. It offers live-in accommodation, work placements and pre-employment training. A centre can be found in each port city in the United Kingdom and most major towns in rural areas.

www.nationalweaselcentres.co.uk

Pay Book: A pocket book that recorded a WCGA soldier's pay. It was red in colour with an acorn on crossed swords with a crown above as the emblem on its front. Until 2008 pay books were produced on weekly parade by WDA soldiers to receive their pay. All pay is now automated through the woodland BACS system.

Pte: Private, the first rank in the WCGA, WDA and SRA that is obtained after basic training. This rank can change between different regiments. Cavalry – Trooper, Artillery – Gunner, however the soldier's position is still the same within the command structure of his army. Troopers and gunners of goat mounted / drawn regiments are considered senior to infantry privates. For example, a Henley-on-Thames Light Cavalry trooper during the rebellion would have been senior to any other Private or Gunner in the WCGA, which would have given him command status when amongst other privates of different regiments, but his rank and pay would still not have exceeded that of a private.

Rifle Creature: Paw soldier in the WCGA and WDA. A rifle creature marches on his paws and is part of a section of other creatures. His purpose is to fight the enemy with his rifle as part of a team under the command of his officers and non-commissioned officers.

Running the belt: With no mains electricity in most tailor's shops, a belt was used to wind a dynamo that produced DC electric current. "The belt", as it was known, was a treadmill which powered sewing machines and other equipment. This employment was only offered to stoats before 1965. Hours on the belt were long and lowly paid. There were no Stoat tailors or cutters in this period. In 1980 mains electric was connected to all domestic burrows and businesses which made this practice obsolete. The woodland rag trade is now part of the "Lets make it fair in woodland" directive that was created in 1978.

RWN: The Royal Woodland Navy.

Sai Jean (pronounced "say jhon"): Woodland slang with the implication "to juggle and to dance" included in its meaning. Once translated simply means, "talk to John". Any unaccompanied female who spoke to a male without introduction before the nineteen eighties was considered to be a prostitute. Frankie Waterwell's hostess bar in Weaselville took this name.

Saint Tickle's: A woodland charity organisation that delivers outreach medical care to all creatures. They have been running for over fifty years. Saint Tickle's medical teams travel and set up dispensaries in the most remote areas of the United Kingdom and deliver medical care and health education.

www.saintickles.co.uk

Section 22: Officially a government department which recruited soldiers under the "1951 Woodland rehabilitation of offenders act" between 1965 and 1977. Unofficially, an élite airborne fighting force that had few boundaries of the rules of engagement. Section 22 is now disbanded but has become legendary because of its large number of recruits from the Yards and HMWP Swindon during the rebellion. "Section 22" was stamped in each soldier's pay book on entry to the WCGA. Many WDA airborne soldiers have Section 22 tattooed on their right shoulder.

Senior Ranks: Any creature of the rank of Sergeant or above

SRA: The Stoat Rebel Army

Soap pressed creases: From world war one onwards the Woodland Army wore serge and wool uniforms (1937 – 1965 Battle Dress) that were difficult to press. Soap was run down the inside of the creases of jackets, then pressed with an iron to achieve a razor-sharp effect. The Woodland Democratic army now uses spray-on starch. Many creatures still say that the whole nature of soldiering in the woodland went downhill and led to undisciplined troops when the battle dress uniform was dropped in 1965 in favour of the French cut, Portuguese pattern combat jacket that only needed to be pressed with a domestic iron.

Trooper: A rank in the WCGA cavalry. Also a much favoured word used by the woodland press during the rebellion, as a derogatory term against the WCGA when they were deployed in operations in areas including a civilian population, e.g. "Acorn's Troopers"

The élite: Hares and Badgers. These creatures before the rebellion held all the key jobs in woodland arts, the police, judiciary and television.

The Yards: Live-in places of work that can be found in each port city of the United Kingdom. The yards provide automobile service and parts, with some yards also catering for marine engines. A fringe life-style, military service and benevolence to the poor, combined with implication in organised woodland and human crime, has brought the creatures who live and work in these establishments, who are mostly weasels and stoats, much notoriety over the years. However, they do accept kittens from the woodland orphanage for work and offer accommodation with a stable family atmosphere and clearly defined social boundaries. During the rebellion the yards on both sides of the conflict opened their gates to the poor on a government agreement. This emergency action by the now disbanded Woodland Central Government and Stoat Rebel Army is still discussed to this day as many creatures of the woodland alleged corruption over this period of woodland history. In real terms the yards saved thousands of lives, but their lifestyle could not be ignored. In 1986 a white bow tie and black dinner jacket that allegedly belonged to Morteki Ben Adam Brock, Foreman of Mingo's Yard in Bristol, was offered as evidence by a human crown prosecution barrister (John Pickles, QC) during the Drinks Mat robbery case. Mingo Waterwell's solicitors J. Vole and company of Clifton, Bristol, provided litigation saying that he was on holiday at Margate in Kent at the time of the robbery and his name was cleared from the case.

Tickle Fish: Freshly caught Minnow, best served with baked beans and chips with a light garnish of lemon or mint.

Ticklemas: A festival between Christmas and New Year where all creatures meet as collective groups, to feast and bow before Pan who visits each group in turn. This is a most holy period for the woodland, but it is also full of presents, tinsel and fairy lights.

WAF: Woodland Air Force.

WBC: Woodland Broadcasting Corporation, which was run by the élite before the rebellion. The WBC still runs today, however it is not as popular as its competitor WITV.

WCGA: The Woodland Central Government Army.
WDA: The Woodland Democratic Army.

WITV: Woodland Independent Television.

Yelk: A twelve stringed instrument with roots going back to pre-medieval times. It is played mostly by stoats, who are masters in the art of woodland music.

.101 rifles: North African manufactured bolt action rifles that had a bore of .101 of an inch. Their maximum range was one hundred yards and took a maximum of five rounds, held in a clip that was pushed down through the breach into a magazine held under the stock. Stoats were often photographed in a practice called "kissing the round" by the woodland press during the rebellion. The SRA said that they did this because of their devotion to the cause of communism. In reality the rounds (ammunition) were packed in cotton that had to be licked off before the clip was charged.